John A. Campbell

Reminiscences and Documents

Relating to the Civil War During the Year 1865

John A. Campbell

Reminiscences and Documents
Relating to the Civil War During the Year 1865

ISBN/EAN: 9783337223212

Printed in Europe, USA, Canada, Australia, Japan

Cover: Foto ©Andreas Hilbeck / pixelio.de

More available books at **www.hansebooks.com**

REMINISCENCES

AND

DOCUMENTS

RELATING TO THE

Civil War During the Year 1865.

By JOHN A. CAMPBELL.

BALTIMORE:

JOHN MURPHY & CO.

1887.

REMINISCENCES AND DOCUMENTS

RELATING TO THE

Civil War During the Year 1865.

M Y object in preparing this paper is to place in order documents that have some historical interest and to record, briefly, some reminiscences relating to events that have interest to those who were concerned in them. The period of time includes some months of the year 1865.

On the 28th of January, 1865, Mr. Benjamin, the Secretary of State in the Confederate government, informed me that the President (Davis) had decided to send a commission to Washington City to confer with the President of the United States upon the subject of peace; that Messrs. A. H. Stephens, R. M. T. Hunter and myself would compose the commission, and that

he came for me to go to the dwelling of the
President to get information and instructions. I
found the persons mentioned convened and President Davis communicated the cause of the commission and the functions which were assigned
to it. He stated that there was exceeding discontent in the United States with the condition
of affairs in Mexico, so much so, that it was
proposed to combine the United States and the
Confederate States to extrude by a union of
their forces the Emperor Maximilian and his
associates and allies.

We were not farther informed of the means
to be used, nor what combination of force was
to be made, nor what was to be done with
Mexico should we succeed. We had the power
(orally) to make any treaty, but one that involved reconstruction of the Federal Union.
President Davis in his book on the Confederate
States, and their Rise and Downfall has not informed us, more particularly, as to these
questions.

Our commission authorized us to have an
informal conference with the President of the
United States upon " the issues involved in the
war existing, with the view of securing peace to
the *two countries.*" The letter written by President Lincoln expressed a continuing disposition
to receive agents commissioned by Mr. Davis to

confer upon the subject of securing peace to the "*People of our one Common Country.*"[1]

There was some detention in our progress—at Petersburg and at City Point—but not unreasonable, for on the third of February, 1865, we were brought face to face with President Lincoln, and Secretary of State Seward, in the cabin of a steamer at anchor in Hampton Roads, to confer informally, as commissioned, on the issues involved in the existing war; and we did confer for several hours, until both parties were satisfied. The intercourse was courteous, and the conversations conducted with gravity and without levity or unfairness. We separated in the afternoon and reported to President Davis the result the fifth of February, 1865, at Richmond, having been absent only eight days. The members of the commission had recognized the propriety of recording their recollection of what had occurred, separately; I did so shortly after my return home, with care. It was submitted to my colleagues and without objection. Mr. Stephens had this when he wrote his histories concerning the war. I am the survivor of all those who participated at the conference. The letter written to Mr. Hunter at his request, the memoranda of

---

[1] 2 Davis' Rise and Downfall, 612–618. Mr. Francis P. Blair was the only person from Mr. Lincoln quoted by Mr. Davis.

the conference, and the report of the commissioners of the result of the conference were drawn by me. These contain all that has been prepared by anyone connected, except what is contained in the message of President Lincoln to the Federal Congress and the documents with it. This message is exact.

The "memoranda" will show that the project relative to the invasion of Mexico, as disclosed by Mr. Stephens, was the subject of conversation, and that Mr. Stephens and Secretary Seward became entangled in a debate which ran into the question of a right of a State to secede. Mr. Lincoln, with a great deal of emphasis and force, hushed the debate by disclaiming all connection or knowledge with Mr. Blair's communications to President Davis. Among the Commissioners, Mr. Stephens alone had any credulity in respect to the suggestion of an arrangement of an invasion of Mexico by the combined forces of the United States and the Confederate States. Mr. Stephens thought it a rational and proper enterprise.

The conference upon the subject of the President's proclamation of emancipation of the slaves in the Southern States, enabled Mr. Seward to inform us of what had been done in Congress since the Commission had been on their journey. The thirteenth amendment to the Constitution had been proposed in Congress, and the resolution had been adopted by the Senate. The two-thirds vote had not been obtained in the House of Representatives. On the 1st day of February, 1865, the two-thirds vote for the first time was obtained, and it was then adopted. Some newspapers informed us that on that day Secretary Seward and Chief Justice Chase were upon the floor of the House soliciting the adoption by the members of the House because it would be useful in the discussion of the subject with the Southern Commissioners, who were to meet Mr. Seward at the Hampton Roads concerning a peace. Mr. Seward took a copy of the record of the adoption of the resolution, and procured its ratification by the Legislature of Maryland at Annapolis.

While we were detained at City Point this amendment to the Constitution had been adopted by Congress and by seven States ratified. A number of members who had opposed the resolution previously had either changed their votes or had absented themselves on this occasion.

Mr. Seward handed me a printed slip stating the action of Congress, being the first information we had of the subject. I enquired of him what significance he attached to it?

He replied: "Not a great deal;" the Southern States will return to the Union, and with their own strength and the aid of the connections they will form with other States, this amendment will be defeated.

I append to this statement

(1). A letter addressed to Mr. Hunter.

(2). A memorandum of the conference at Hampton Roads.

(3). A copy of the report made to the President of the Confederate States.

(1). Letter to Hon. R. M. T. Hunter.

169 St. Paul Street, Baltimore,
31st *October*, 1877.

My Dear Sir:

Your letter of the 28th instant has been received, and I proceed to comply with your request. The Commissioners appointed in 1865 to confer with the President of the United States concerning Peace were furnished with a letter addressed to Mr. Francis P. Blair by President Lincoln, wherein the latter consented to receive persons coming from those in authority in the Southern States, who desired to make peace on the basis "of *one common country.*" This letter we were to exhibit at the lines of the Federal armies, and told it would serve us as a passport to Washington City.

The letters of appointment for the Commissioners, and I believe the treasure with which our expenses were to be borne, were delivered to me by Mr. Washington, of the State Department of the Confederate States, at night, after our interview with the Executive. I noticed to Mr. Washington the letter of appointment did not correspond to the letter of Mr. Lincoln to Mr. Blair, and that this might make difficulty.

I learned from him there had been a discussion and a difference between Mr. Davis and Mr. Benjamin on the subject, and it had been so settled. We left the morning after, and I gave to Mr. Stephens and to yourself the papers on the way to Petersburg.

There was detention at Petersburg. The Federal officers did not understand our passport, if I may so call it, and had to apply to Washington City. While awaiting instructions, and within two or three days after our departure, General Grant allowed us to go to City Point, his headquarters. Within two days or more Colonel Eckert, an officer of the United States, arrived at City Point from Washington City. He had a copy of the letter from President Lincoln to Mr. Blair. With General Grant he came to us, and enquired whether we accepted the conditions of the letter he bore, and which we had been advised of and furnished with.

The only answer we could make was to submit our letter of appointment to observation. The discrepancy between obtaining a peace on the basis of " one common country," and a peace " between *two* countries," was pointed out, and we were told we could not proceed. We argued that peace was desirable and desired, and that the information sought was how peace was to be had. I remember our friend, Mr. Stephens, suggested that neither note was accurate, for that thirty-six countries (States) were involved. General Grant and Colonel Eckert retired and conferred, and were most emphatic in their refusal after this information. We addressed one, and perhaps more letters, to those officers, to change the resolution so that the expedition might not be wholly abortive or without result.

During the night following General Grant visited the Commissioners, and sat with Mr. Stephens and yourself for some time. I was sick and not present.

As a consequence of his intercourse he telegraphed President Lincoln favorably in respect to the conference, and recommended that he should see the Commissioners. The following day, perhaps, we heard that a conference would

2

take place at Hampton Roads, and, perhaps, on the day after the conference took place.

The correspondence of the Commissioners, the report of General Grant, and the result of the conference were communicated to the Congress of the United States by President Lincoln in February, 1865. By a reference to these the dates may be seen. I speak only from memory.

At Hampton Roads Mr. Stephens, with clearness and precision, stated the conditions we had been instructed to place before the President and the dispositions we had in respect to them, and which we had supposed were more or less settled upon.

President Lincoln disclaimed all knowledge of any such proposed conditions, denied having given any sort of authority to any one to hold out any expectations of any arrangements of the kind being made, and declared that he would listen to no proposition which did not include an immediate recognition of the National authority in all the States and the abandonment of resistance to it.

I confess that these answers did not surprise me, and that any other would have filled me with amazement.

> Very truly, your friend,
>
> (Signed,)   JOHN A. CAMPBELL.

HON. R. M. T. HUNTER,
    Richmond, Va.

Explanation.

The foregoing letter was furnished to Mr. Hunter. It was published by him in connection with correspondence between him and Mr. Davis in the papers of the Southern Historical Society. I use it merely as a statement of the facts recorded in it.

> (Signed,)   J. A. C.

(2). MEMORANDUM OF THE CONVERSATION AT THE CON-
FERENCE IN HAMPTON ROADS.

The conference was opened by some conversation between
Mr. Stevens and President Lincoln relative to their connection as members of a committee or association to promote the
election of General Taylor as President in 1848.

The composition of the association, the fate of different
members (Truman Smith and Mr. Toombs and others)—the
time that the parties had served in Congress together, when
Mr. Hunter and Mr. Seward became members of the Senate,
and other personal incidents were alluded to.

After this the parties approached the subject of the conference.

At a very early stage in the conversation Mr. Lincoln
announced with some emphasis that until the National authority be recognized within the Confederate States, that no
consideration of any other terms or conditions could take
place.

Mr. Stephens then suggested if there might not be some
plan devised by which that question could be adjourned, and
to let its settlement await the calm that would occur in the
passions and irritations that the war had created. That it
was important to divert the public mind from the present
quarrel to some matters to which the parties had a common
feeling and interest, and mentioned the condition of Mexico
as affording such an opportunity. Mr. Lincoln answered that
the settlement of the existing difficulties was of supreme importance, and that he was not disposed to entertain any proposition for an armistice or cessation of hostilities until they were
determined by the re-establishment of the National authority
over the United States—that he had considered the question
of an armistice fully—he would not consent to a proposition
of the kind.

Mr. Campbell asked in what manner was reconstruction to

be effected, supposing that the Confederate authorities were consenting to it?

Mr. Seward requested that the answer to this question might be deferred until Mr. Stevens could develop his ideas more fully as they had a philosophical basis. He had proposed to divert the mind from the existing troubles.

Mr. Stephens then proceeded at some length to express his opinions upon the so-called Monroe doctrine and his assent to it. That the establishment of an empire in Mexico was in hostility to that doctrine, and was offence against the Confederate States as much as against the United States. That he was favorable to the appropriation of the whole of the North American continent by the States of the two Confederacies, and exclude foreigners from a control over it. That there might be a union of power for that object, and in the course of that union fraternal feelings would arise and a settlement might be acceptably made. That the conquest of Mexico would introduce a new element and would require modifications of the existing system, etc.

Mr. Seward interposed and made enquiries as to what would be the *status quo* during the period employed in the consummation of this enterprise? He referred to the managements concerning the tariffs—the government of the territory of the Confederate States in the occupation of the respective authorities—the case when two governments existed in the same State, one recognized by the United States, and the other by the Confederacy.

This was answered by statements that a military convention might be entered into which would provide for all these subjects.

That the troops on either side might be withdrawn into ascertained stations or ports, and that the duties collected might be arranged in the agreement, and that the government of the State recognized by the Confederacy should be supreme in the States. This branch of the discussion was closed by Mr. Lincoln who answered—that it could not be entertained.

That there could be no war without the consent of Congress, and no treaty without the consent of the Senate of the United States. That he could make no treaty with the Confederate States because that would be a recognition of those States, and that this could not be done under any circumstances. That unless a settlement were made there would be danger that the quarrel would break out in the midst of the joint operations. That one party might unite with the common enemy to destroy the other. That he was determined to do nothing to suspend the operations for bringing the existing struggle to a close to attain any collateral end.

Mr. Lincoln in this part of the conversation admitted that he had power to make a military convention, and that his arrangements under that might extend to settle several points mentioned, but others it could not. The question was renewed as to how the reconstruction was to be accomplished, supposing that the Confederate States were consenting?

He answered—by disbanding the troops and permitting the National authorities to resume their functions.

Mr. Seward said : That Mr. Lincoln could not express himself more aptly than he had done in his message to Congress in December last, and recited a portion of that message and specified the mode by saying that where there was a custom house, that officer would be appointed to collect duties, and appointments to the postoffice, courts, land offices, etc., etc., should be made, and the laws submitted to. It was replied that the separation and the war had given rise to questions and interests which it would be necessary to provide for by stipulations, and to adjust before a restoration of former relations could be efficiently made. That the disbandment of the army was a delicate and difficult operation, and that time was needed for this. That confiscation Acts had been passed, and property sold under them, and the title would be affected by the facts existing when the war ended unless provided for by the stipulation.

The reply to this was, that as to all questions involving

rights of property, the Courts could determine them, and that Congress would no doubt be liberal in making restitution of confiscated property, or by indemnity, after the passions that had been excited by the war had been composed.

Special reference was made to the effects of the President's Proclamation of Emancipation of slaves. He said that there were different opinions as to its operation. That some believed that it was not operative at all : others, that it operated only within the circle which had been occupied by the army, and others believed that it was operative everywhere in the States to which it applied. That this would be decided when cases arose: that he could not modify any part of it.

Mr. Seward produced the proposed amendment to the Constitution that had been adopted the 31st of January, and which had not been seen by the Commissioners.

He said : that these were passed as a war measure, and under the predominance of revolutionary passion, and if the war were ended, it was probable that the measures of war would be abandoned.

He alluded to the power of such passions in precipitating emancipation measures in Maryland and Missouri. That the most extreme views in a revolution were sure to acquire predominance, and that the more moderate parties were always overborne, as they were in those States.

Mr. Hunter spoke of the cruelty of such measures to the slave population, especially in localities in which the men had been removed. That the women and children were a tax upon their masters, and if emancipated, would be helpless and suffering.

To this Mr. Lincoln replied with a story, of a man who had planted potatoes for his hogs, and left them in the ground to be rooted for; the ground froze, but the master said the hogs must root nevertheless.

Mr. Seward was asked if he supposed the slavery agitation would end with emancipation? If there would not be agitation as to the status of the slave? He assented that it was quite possible. Mr. Hunter enquired of Mr. Lincoln, if the State of Virginia were to return to the Union, would it be with her ancient limits? The answer to this was, that the question would have to be settled by other departments of the Government, but that, in his opinion, Western Virginia would remain as she is.

In the course of the conversation Mr. Hunter remarked that there had been numerous instances in which parties to contests, similar to this, had conferred through Commissioners, and had made agreements in reference to matters in dispute, and instanced the case of Charles I and the Parliament of Great Britain. Mr. Lincoln replied, "all he knew of Charles I, was, that he lost his head." To another instance cited by Mr. Stephens in another connection, he expressed unfeignedly his ignorance of history, and referred him to Mr. Seward, for that kind of discussion. In conclusion Mr. Hunter summed up what seemed to be the result of the interview.

That there would be no arrangement by treaty between the Confederate States and the United States, or any agreements between them. That there was nothing left for them, but unconditional submission. Mr. Seward remarked that they had not used the word submission or any word that implied humiliation to the States, and begged that it should not be noted. Mr. Lincoln, in the course of his remarks, had said, that the laws relative to confiscation and pains and penalties, had left the matter in his hands, and that he could express himself freely as to them. That he would say, that the power granted to him would be very liberally exerted. That he could not answer what Congress would do, as to the admission of members of Congress. That it was their business to decide upon that, and that they had rejected members who, in his opinion, ought to have been admitted. Reference was made to Mr. Blair. It was said by Mr. Lincoln, that doubtless the old man meant well, but that he had given him no authority to make any proposition or statement to any one. That he had stopped him from proceeding when he commenced to tell him of his business in Richmond.

Mr. Hunter stated that in candor he should say that upon the subject of Mexico, there was a diversity of opinion in the Confederate States, and that it was not probable that any arrangement could be made for her invasion without much opposition.

Mr. Seward had evidently encouraged Mr. Stephens in his remarks upon the general subject, and sympathized apparently in his general views, and represented that there was a very strong feeling in the Northern States on this subject. He or Mr. Lincoln had remarked that there never was a question upon which the Northern mind seemed to be more harmonious.

Upon the observation of Mr. Hunter before stated, they qualified what had been previously said on that subject, and stated that there was a strong feeling in the North, that the affairs in Mexico were not right, and that something ought to be done.

Mr. Seward remarked that their foreign relations were complicated, and that the feeling of the United States was as strong against England as against France. That they were in the situation that they were in, prior to the war of 1812. With a cause of war against both nations, and uncertain against which to proceed. That it might be, that they would be decided by the ancient grudge against Great Britain.

I have stated the import of the conference generally, without introducing what was said by the different members of the commission, except when their remarks were direct and pointed to some particular subject.

My own purpose was to ascertain, if possible, the precise views of Messrs. Lincoln and Seward, as to the manner in which reconstruction would be effected, and the rights that would be secured to the Southern States in the event that one should take place.

I expressed the opinion that an agreement to go upon an enterprise against Mexico, leaving the strongholds of the Confederacy in the hands of the enemy, would lead inevitably to reconstruction.   Mr. Hunter expressed the opinion that it might lead to independence with a close alliance, sufficient to arrange satisfactorily all questions of trade and intercourse, and for defence against foreign aggression.

Both agreed that in the present temper of both nations, that a re-union would not be profitable to either, and should not be desired by either.   Mr. Seward at one time said, that the Northern States were weary of war, and would be willing to pay what they would probably be required to pay on account of its continuance, but did not explain himself further on this subject.

Mr. Lincoln stated that he regarded the North to be as much responsible for slavery as the South, and that he would be rejoiced to be taxed on his little property for indemnities to the masters of slaves.   Mr. Seward remarked that the North had already paid on that account.

These observations were incidently made and did not seem to have any reference to the general subject.   They were not intended apparently as the ground of any proposition.

Mr. Stephens requested President Lincoln to reconsider his conclusions upon the subject of a suspension of hostilities.

Mr. Lincoln replied that he would reconsider it as asked, but as at present advised he could not promise any consent to such a proposal: that he had maturely considered of the plan, and determined that it could not be done.

At the commencement of the conference, it was understood that it was to be free and open, that none of the parties were to be held to anything that was said, and that the whole was to be in confidence.

(Signed,)   J. A. CAMPBELL.

February, 1865.

3

(3). Report of the Commissioners.

To the President of the Confederate States:

Under your letter of appointment of the 28th ultimo, we proceeded to seek an informal conference with Abraham Lincoln, President of the United States, upon the subject mentioned in the letter. The conference was granted and took place on the 3rd inst., on board of a steamer anchored in Hampton Roads, where we met President Lincoln and the Hon. Mr. Seward, Secretary of State of the United States. It continued for several hours and was both full and explicit. We learned from them that the message of President Lincoln to the Congress of the United States in December last explains clearly and distinctly his sentiments as to the terms, conditions and methods of proceeding by which peace can be secured to the people, and we were not informed that they would be modified or altered to obtain that end. We understood from him that no terms or proposals of any treaty or agreement looking to an ultimate settlement would be entertained, or made by him with the authorities of the Confederate States, because that would be a recognition of their existence as a separate power, which under no circumstances would be done; and for a like reason, that no such terms would be entertained by him for the States separately; that no extended truce or armistice (as at present advised) would be granted or allowed without a satisfactory assurance in advance of the complete restoration of the authority of the Constitution and laws of the United States over all places within the States of the Confederacy; that whatever consequences may follow from the re-establishment of that authority must be accepted; but that individuals subject to pains and penalties under the laws of the United States might rely upon a very liberal use of the power confided to him to remit those pains and penalties if peace be restored. During the conference the proposed amendment to the Constitution of the United States adopted by Congress on the 31st ultimo was brought to our notice.

This amendment provided that neither slavery nor involuntary servitude, except for crime, should exist within the United States or any place within their jurisdiction, and that Congress should have power to enforce this amendment by appropriate legislation.

Very respectfully, etc.,

(Signed,)   ALEXANDER H. STEPHENS,
R. M. T. HUNTER,
JOHN A. CAMPBELL.

The report made to the President of the Confederate States by the commissioners was received with expressions of surprise in Richmond,—and then of indignation, disdain, denunciation, defiance. A mass meeting was held within a few days in one of the churches at mid-day where all of these expressions were echoed. The President, Secretary of State, and prominent Congressmen participating in the meeting. The public feelings were excited and pledges were given that the war would be continued to the last extremity. The public hope was encouraged and stimulated; but this was of short duration. The march of events had become quick and their progress subdual. The army of General Sherman had crossed the Savannah River into South Carolina, and the cities and towns of Branchville, Charleston, Columbia, Cheraw, Fayetteville and Wilmington were captured and marauded. Sheridan completed another raid north of the

James River, and the James River Canal and other works were dilapidated, and his cavalry rejoined the Army of the Potomac.

The Army of the Potomac which had reached the James River several months before with so much of difficulty and such enormous losses, had been recruited so as to number more than it had been at any time before. It had every equipment, and all supports and supplies which could impart strength or infuse confidence of success. The Army of Northern Virginia at this date was destitute of much which was important, even to the ordinary support of an army upon which no responsibility rests, or from which no arduous service is expected. During the autumn of 1864, the hospitals, workshops, factories, plantations; the rolls of exempts, and of men detailed, were diligently examined to find persons to perform military duty without accomplishing any effective result. At the commencement of 1865, there was no connection between the government in Richmond and the Trans-Mississippi department; the defeat of the army at Nashville had opened the West and the South-west to invasion in every part; Sherman's army had devastated Georgia, and all the railroad communications in the South and South-west. The war was on the part of the Confederates limited to the defence of Richmond and its dependencies. The army of General

Sherman was moving toward Richmond, and another army was moving from Wilmington.

The war had so diminished the resources of the Confederacy to recruit their armies was not practicable. A Northern report informs us that the Confederate DEAD amounted to 133,821 of men killed in battle or who had died in hospital; the prisoners paroled on the field amounted to 248,599. There were in Northern prisons soldiers able to supply three armies as large as the Army of Northern Virginia. The Army of Northern Virginia after January, 1865, could not obtain recruits west of the Savannah river. At that date the United States had more of colored troops enlisted than the Confederate States had in the field in Virginia and the Carolinas. The state of the Commissariat had been a subject of anxiety during all of the war. Congress did not, until the month of March, 1865, pass any law to take possession and control of the railroads.

The blockade during the first years of the war was easily evaded. The reports of a few cases in the English law reports show that the profits were marvellous. One vessel (the Robert E. Lee) in a few months saved the Confederate States about $30,000,000 of their currency.

Finally the blockade was complete. The Confederacy suffered because of the inferiority of arms, munition, clothing, medicines, and hospital stores and other necessaries. The destruction of animals impaired the cavalry and artillery service. There was, in my opinion, full justification for the opinion that peace on the precise terms offered at the Hampton Roads Conference, if none better could be obtained, should have been accepted. The precise grounds assumed by the executive department was that nothing could be done on the basis disclosed in the report for want of any authority on the part of the Confederate administration. A convention of the States could not be assembled by any means within the reach of the Government of the Confederacy at this period.

Without any consultation with the Secretary of War (General John C. Breckenridge), I addressed to him a letter dated 5th March, 1865, after hearing from the deputation or committee of Senators the conclusion of the President. The Committee was composed of Messrs. Orr, Hunter, Barnwell, and W. A. Graham—two Senators from South Carolina, one from Virginia, and one from North Carolina. These were all men of conspicuous ability and character. A copy of this letter I have submitted attached to this paper. With the letter addressed to the Secretary of War there was evidence of the entire exhaustion of the Treasury department, and a copy of the memoranda of the Hampton Roads Conference.

LETTER TO WILLIAM A. GRAHAM.[1]

WAR DEPARTMENT, 24*th February*, 1865.

HON. WILLIAM A. GRAHAM,
Senate of the Confederate States:

I understand the position of Mr. Lincoln to be that he will not make any treaty or agreement with the Confederate States, but only that he will treat or confer with individuals resisting the National authority, and will declare to them the terms on which he will make an adjustment. I do not consider that this position of his will prevent the settlement of the conditions.

In any event the action of Congress (U. S.) might be required to carry into effect the stipulations, and whether these are informally agreed to, or are formally made, it is presumed will not make a wide difference in the final result.

The stipulations that the President can settle under his powers as President, it is material to consider. He is the Commander-in-Chief of the Army, and has exercised a large share of power as such; he has the power of pardon by the Constitution, and the Acts of Confiscation provide: "That the President may, by proclamation, extend to persons who may have participated in the existing rebellion in any State, or part thereof, pardon and amnesty, with such exceptions and on such conditions as he may deem expedient for the public welfare." The Act of Congress of the United States of the 16th day of July, 1862, embodies the principle of the provisions that have been made to Confiscation.

This Act provides: That to insure the speedy termination of the present rebellion, it shall be the duty of the President

---

[1] This letter was written to answer the specific question, what besides the reconstruction of the Union and the emancipation of the slaves was involved as legal consequences of a total defeat in the field of battle.

of the United States to cause the seizure of all the estate and property, moneys, stocks, credits and effects of the persons mentioned, and to apply the same and the proceeds thereof to the use of the army. The proceedings are to be in rem in any District Court of the United States, or in the District of Columbia, and the property to be sold under decrees of condemnation.

There is another Act on this subject upon captured and abandoned property, and provides for its sale, &c., &c., and that the party interested may reclaim the proceeds after the war upon proof of loyalty.

I think the effect of amnesty would be to relieve all property from the operation of the law of confiscation. My impression is that it would have the effect to destroy the judicial sales made under it. These sales were made before any conviction, and without service of process, on the party, and it is difficult to realize how the Act can be supported against one claimed to be a citizen, and whose loyalty is vouched by a Presidential pardon.

In this connection all fines and penalties incurred by any visitation of revenue laws would have to be considered, and a release from arrears of taxes and duties. A clause in the Act of 7th of June, 1862, is to this effect : " That the title of and into each parcel of land upon which said tax has not been paid as above provided, shall thereupon become forfeited to the United States and upon the sale thereafter shall vest in the United States, or in the purchasers in said sale in fee simple, free and discharged from all prior liens, incumbrances, right, title and dues whatsoever."

There are some conditions precedent to the operation of this Section of the Act which, perhaps, have not yet been fulfilled, but another Section imposes a lien upon the lands which does not depend upon any condition.

The arrears of taxes for three years, and the stringent conditions of the Act, will occasion the forfeiture of a large amount of property for taxes if the collection of the arrears is insisted on.

The legislation upon the subject of slavery in the District of Columbia, in the territories, forts, arsenals and the repealing of the fugitive slave Acts. Besides these there is an Act to liberate all slaves in places captured by the United States, and the penal provisions of several of the Acts of Congress provide specially for the emancipation of slaves of the owner.

Western Virginia was admitted to the Union in 1862, in December. It purports to have been done upon the consent of the people of that section, and of the Legislature of the State.

In a number of the States, the public lands have been appropriated by the State, as Florida, Alabama, Mississippi, Louisiana and Arkansas, and in others a portion of the public money of the United States was seized.

I suppose that an arrangement as to these would be required. The commissioner being empowered to settle the terms of peace upon the recognition of the national authority, would have to consider very carefully the laws that have been made since July 1st, 1861. Besides these arrangements, the disbanding of the army ; the adjustment of the public debt ; the disposition of the public property ; the admission of the States into fellowship ; the suppression of governments that have grown

4

up during the war, and affairs connected with the internal policy of the States should command attention. I cannot see that order can be fully restored, without a long interval between the decision to reconstruct the Union, and the consummation of that act.

I question whether this will be agreed to, but wise statesmanship clearly indicates that it would be better that this should be adopted as the mode of procedure.

Very respectfully,

(Signed,)   J. A. CAMPBELL.

LETTER TO GENERAL J. C. BRECKENRIDGE.

WAR DEPARTMENT, RICHMOND,

March 5th, 1865.

GENERAL J. C. BRECKENRIDGE,

Secretary of War.

Sir :—

The present condition of the country requires, in my opinion, that a full and exact examination be made into the resources of the Confederate Government available for the approaching campaign, and that accurate views of our situation be taken.

It is not the part of statesmanship to close our eyes upon them.

The most important of these is the state of the finances. This department is in debt from four to five hundred millions of dollars. The service of all of its bureaus is paralyzed by want of money and credit.

The estimates for this year amount to $1,048,858,275. This only includes an estimate of six months for the Commissary Department, and excludes 135,000 pounds sterling for the nitre and mining service. These being included, the estimate would be $1,338,858,275 Confederate notes. The currency is, at the Treasury valuation 60 to 1 as compared with coin, and when the small stock of coin in the Treasury is expended, and the sales of which now control the market, no one can foretell the extent of the depreciation that will ensue.

It is needless to comment on these facts.

2. Second only to the question of finance, and perhaps of equal importance, is the condition of the armies as to men. In April, 1862, the revolutionary measure of conscription was resorted to, the men between 18 and 35 were then placed in service. The eventful campaign of 1862 compelled the addition of the class between 35 and 40 to the call of April. The campaign that terminated in July, 1863, with the loss of Vicksburg, and the disaster at Gettysburg, made a call for the men between 40 and 45 necessary. In February, 1864, the Conscript Act was made more stringent, and the population between 17 and 50 were made subject to call. At the same time, the currency was reduced one-third by taxation and heavy taxes were laid otherwise.

In October, 1864, all details of men for particular service were revoked. The casualties of war cannot be accurately ascertained, but enough is known to show that no large addition can be made from the conscript population. General Preston reports "that there are over 100,000 deserters scattered over the Confederacy. That so common is the crime, it has in popular estimation lost the stigma which justly pertains to it, and therefore the criminals are everywhere shielded by their families, and by the sympathies of many communities."

The States of North Carolina, South Carolina, Georgia, and perhaps others, have passed laws to withdraw from service men liable to it under existing laws, and these laws have the support of local authorities. I think that the number of deserters is, perhaps, overstated, but the evil is one of enormous magnitude, and the means of the department to apply a corrective have diminished in proportion to its increase.

I do not regard the slave population as a source from which an addition to the army can be successfully derived. If the use of slaves had been resorted to in the beginning of the war, for service in the Engineer Troops and as teamsters and laborers, it might have been judicious. Their employment since 1862 has been difficult and latterly almost impracticable.

The attempt to collect 20,000 men has been obstructed and rendered nearly abortive. The enemy have raised about as many from the fugitives occasioned by the draft as ourselves from its execution. General Holmes reports 1,500 fugitives in one week in North Carolina. Colonel Blount reported a desertion of 1,210 last summer in Mobile, and Governor Clarke, of Mississippi, entreats the suspension of the call for them in that State.

As a practical measure, I cannot see how a slave force can be collected, armed and equipped at the present time.

In immediate connection with this subject is that of subsistence for the army. This has been attended with difficulty since the commencement of the war, in consequence of want of efficient control over the transportation, and the difficulty of funds. There were abundant supplies in the country at that time, and the transportation was fully adequate, but these were not under control. The Treasury has never answered the full demands of the Commissary Department with promptitude. These difficulties were aggravated when the currency became depreciated, and prices were determined by commissioners, so as to lighten the burden upon the Treasury and without reference to the market.

They have been still more aggravated by the subjugation of the most productive parts of the country, the devastation of other portions, and the destruction of railroads. Production has been diminished, and the quantity of supplies has been so much reduced that under the most favorable circumstances subsistence for the army would not be certain and adequate.

At present these embarrassments have become so much accumulated that the late Commissary General pronounces the problem of subsistence of the Army of Northern Virginia, in its present position, insoluble, and the present Commissary General requires the fulfilment of conditions, though not unreasonable, nearly impossible.

5. The remarks upon the subject of subsistence are applicable to the clothing, fuel and forage requisite for the army service, and in regard to the supplies of animals for cavalry and artillery service. The transportation by railroad south of this city is now limited to the Danville railroad. The present capacity of that road is insufficient to bring supplies adequate to the support of the Army of Northern Virginia, and the continuance of that road, even at its existing conditions, cannot be relied on. It can render no assistance in facilitating the movements of troops.

6. The Chief of Ordnance reports that he has a supply of 25,000 arms. He has been dependent on a foreign market for one-half of the arms used. This source is nearly cut off. His workshops, in many instances, have been destroyed, and those in use have been impaired by the withdrawal of details. He calls loudly for the withdrawal of men from the army to re-establish the efficiency of some of them. There is reason to apprehend that the most important of the manufactories of arms will be destroyed in a short time, and we have to contemplate a deficiency of arms and ammunition.

7. The foregoing observations apply to the Nitre and Mining Bureau, and the Medical Department is not in a better condition than the other bureaus. The armies in the field in North Carolina and Virginia do not afford encouragement to prolong resistance.

General Lee reported a few days ago the desertion of some 1,200 veteran soldiers. Desertions have been frequent during the whole season, and the *morale* of the army is somewhat impaired. The causes have been abundant for this. Exposed to the most protracted and violent campaign that is known in history, contending against overwhelming numbers, badly equipped, fed, paid, and cared for in camp and hospital, with families suffering at home, this army has exhibited the noblest qualities. It sees everywhere else disasters and defeat, and that their toils and sufferings have been unproductive. The Army of North Carolina can scarcely be regarded as an army. General Johnston has at Charlotte less than 3,000 dispirited and disorganized troops, composed of brigades that are not as large as companies should be. General Hardee has a mixed command; only a small portion of it is efficient. The troops from the Tennessee have not arrived, and we can not hope that they will arrive in good condition.

9. The political condition is not more favorable. Georgia is in a state that may be properly called insurrectionary against the Confederate authorities. Her public men of greatest influence have cast reproach upon the laws of the Confederacy and the Confederate authorities, and have made the execution of the laws nearly impossible. A mere mention of the condition in Tennessee, Missouri, Kentucky, Western Virginia, and the line of the Mississippi, the seaboard from the Potomac to the Sabine and North Alabama, is necessary. North Carolina is divided, and her divisions prevent her from taking upon herself the support of the war, as Virginia has done. With the evacuation of Richmond the State of Virginia must be abandoned. The war will cease to be a national one from that time.

You cannot but have perceived how much of the treasure, of the hopes and affections of the people of all the States, has been deposited in Virginia, and how much the national spirit has been upheld by the operations here. When this exchequer becomes exhausted, I fear that we shall be bankrupt, and that the public spirit in the South and South-western States will fail.

It is the province of statesmanship to consider of these things.

The South may succumb, but it is not necessary that she should be destroyed. I do not regard reconstruction as involving destruction, unless our people should forget the incidents of their heroic struggle and become debased and degraded. It is the duty of their statesmen and patriots to guard them in the future with even more care and tenderness than they have done in the past. There is anarchy in the opinions of men here, and few are willing to give counsel, and still fewer are willing to incur the responsibility of taking or advising action. In these circumstances I have surveyed the whole ground, I believe calmly and dispassionately. The picture I do not think has been too highly colored. I do not ask that my views be accepted, but that a candid inquiry be made with a view to action. I recommend that General Lee be requested to give his opinion upon the condition of the country, upon a submission of these facts, and that the President submit the subject to the Senate, or to Congress, and invite their action.

Very respectfully, your obedient servant,

(Signed,)   JOHN A. CAMPBELL,
Assistant Secretary of War.

At the same time there was delivered to the Secretary of War a copy of the Memorandum of the Conference at Hampton Roads, made by me; also, an endorsement of Mr. Trenholm, Secretary of the Treasury, to the effect that he had exhausted all of the authority to issue treasury notes, the 31st of December, 1864, and had been selling gold since, to supply urgent wants. That when the supply of gold had been disposed of, the operations of the treasury must close. The amount on hand on the 19th of February was only $750,000.

This statement of the Secretary was made to the President of the Confederate States, upon application of the Quartermaster General for $100,000, to purchase horses and equipments for the artillery, which he represented to be indispensable. The President declined to make the appropriation of the sum asked for.

(Signed,)   J. A. C.

The subsequent history is that General J. C. Breckenridge, after the letter and documents had been explained and delivered to him, required of all the Chiefs of Bureaus in the Department to report to him the condition of his Department, and his ability to fulfil the demands likely to be made.

The Quartermaster General, the Commissary General, so the Chiefs of Ordnance, Nitre and Mining and Conscription, General Lee, Commander-in-Chief of the Armies in the Field, was also required to do so. Each one of these made his report, and some a supplemental report, because of changes in the conditions.

The letter of General Lee was clear and explicit. Referring to the state of his Commissariat, his inability to help himself to a single ration for his army, his absolute dependence on Richmond; referring to the exhausted and enfeebled armies of Johnston, Hardee, Hood, Taylor, and their inability to meet the demands on them. He said that his condition was such that, if it were not greatly improved, he could neither hold his lines before Richmond, nor could he move with his army from them.

These returns were submitted by the Secretary of War to the President. They were the subject of discussion, and were then enclosed in an envelope and submitted to the Congress at its last meetings, about the 14th of March, 1865. There was no discussion there, and the message was probably subsequently captured.

General Weitzell, the commander who entered Richmond, stated to the writer that he had captured it.

The resolution of Mr. Rives was held by Senator Graham, of North Carolina, who assented to the conditions of supreme and unreasoning necessity which existed, and that there was no time to be lost. The night of the adjournment he returned that paper to me, and informed me that the Senators had said that were the resolution to be passed there would be no action taken, and so that nothing could be done of advantage.

(Signed,)   J. A. CAMPBELL.

THE RESOLUTION OF MR. WILLIAM C. RIVES, OF VIRGINIA.

The Senate of the Confederate States, cherishing with undiminished attachment the cause of national independence, but convinced by a careful and conscientious study of their situation, compared with the overwhelming numbers and unlimited resources of their adversary, increased by accessions from every part of Europe, and favored by the partial and unjust policy of foreign powers, that a longer prosecution of the war with any reasonable prospect of success on their part has become impracticable; and yielding, as the proudest and most valiant of nations have done in like circumstances to the stern law of necessity, and the apparent decrees of Heaven; do, in order to prevent a farther and unavailing effusion of blood, to husband the lives and interests of so many of their fellow-citizens committed to their guardianship, and avert the horrors of a savage and relentless subjugation by a triumphant armed force of every race and complexion, advise the President to propose to the enemy through the General-in-Chief, an armistice, preliminary to the re-establishment of peace and union, and for the special purpose of settling and ascertaining certain points incident thereto, to restoration of the Union, and particularly

5

whether the seceded States on their return, will be secured in their rights and privileges as States, under the Constitution of the United States.

The foregoing was endorsed as follows: " This resolution was prepared by William C. Rives, of Virginia." It was handed by me (J. A. C.) to William A. Graham, to be offered to the Senate of the Confederate States, and returned to me without being offered. Mr. Rives prepared it at my request, and it had connection with the letter to General Breckenridge written by me and which Mr. Rives approved.

I delivered the letter to the Secretary of War who adopted the counsel that it contained. He addressed a letter to General Lee, and to each of the Chiefs of Bureaus in the Department of War, viz: the Adjutant-General, Quartermaster-General, Commissary-General, Chief of Ordnance, &c.

1. General Lee answered in effect: The situation is full of peril and difficulty and required prompt action. He stated that he had gleaned the territory within the reach of his army transportation, and was wholly dependent upon the officers at Richmond for his supplies. He could not assist them to collect supplies; they knew better than he did what could be done. But, that if his situation was not greatly improved, he could neither hold his lines before Richmond nor could he remove from them; that he had no exact reports of the situation of General Johnston's army in North Carolina. He thought

it had not been fully organized, but he feared it was not adequate to fulfil the demand upon it. That General Taylor's army was insufficient to perform the duties incumbent on it.

2. The Quartermaster-General answered that, the Richmond and Danville Railroad was his main dependence for the transportation of supplies; that the capacity of that road was barely sufficient to enable him to maintain the army and city of Richmond; that if it was confided to him for that purpose only, he thought it could be done; but if withdrawn, to aid in the movement of troops or other uses, he should not be able to do so. With the papers, an application to the President to direct the use of $100,000 in gold to the purchase of horses and harness for the artillery service; that treasury notes were uncurrent and other provisions must be made. The President referred it to the Secretary of the Treasury; the Secretary answered, that on the 31st December, 1864, he had issued the entire sum which he was authorized to issue. That since that date he had purchased Confederate notes to meet the most urgent demands, at the rate of sixty dollars for one in gold. That when the stock of gold was exhausted his department must close. That he had only $750,000.

3. The Commissary-General (St. John) answered that there were commissary supplies in the terri-

tory within the lines of Richmond; Goldsborough,
North Carolina; Charlotte, North Carolina, and
Staunton, Virginia. That were this territory protected so that his officers and agents might move
easily and purchase, and have sufficient local and
railroad transportation and be furnished with *gold*,
he could perform *the work* of collecting supplies
for the army and the city of Richmond.

4. The Chief of Ordnance and the Surgeon-
General referred to the effect of the exclusion of
intercourse with foreign nations and the grave
inconvenience of the closure of our own ports to
them. The Chief of Ordnance also represented
the damage that had happened to his service by
the orders revoking the details of the men who
had been engaged for duty in his department.
His supply of arms was reduced to 25,000 stand.

5. The Treasury Report for the year 1864 was
withdrawn from the Congress, and the Secretary
in the conditions which existed disclosed a hope-
less state of insolvency. The President in his
last message in March, 1865, exhibits very clearly
that the Treasury could not be set up. There
was no treasure wherewith to fill it, or even to
veil its nudity. The purse, and the arsenal, and
the camp, and magazine, and conscript recruits,
were all wanting in the Confederate States. A
philosopher and historian of this time records:
"A political party that knows not *when it is beaten,*

may become one of the fatalest of things to itself and to all." The same philosopher says, " O patriotism! It was from of old said, 'The loser pays.' It is he who has to pay all scores, run up by whomsoever; on him must all breakages and charges fall." We have proved these aphorisms.

The paper issues that went forth from the Treasury, probably amounted to two billions and upwards. It is probable that there had been *no* payments to the men of the army for two years. General Kirby Smith from the Trans-Mississippi department sent a single requisition of $60,000,000 in September, 1864. The answer to him NO EFFECTS. The purpose of the letter addressed to Secretary Breckenridge was to ascertain whether Congress might not find in the lines of the Constitution a power to make a peace when the necessity appeared. The testimony was collected where information could certainly be found, and which was certainly trustworthy.

It was submitted in advance to the head of the War Department, and to several of the most enlightened statesmen in the Confederate States.

The Secretary of War caused the papers to be submitted to the Cabinet of the President. They were placed in an envelope endorsed " Secret Message of Congress."

There was no statement of this testimony nor reference to it in the President's Message. There was quite an elaborate message sent at the same time, probably, to the same secret session. This message reviews with vigor and asperity the conduct of the Congress, and finds some things had been undone that were of imperative necessity to the public safety, and should have been done.

This message was referred to a select committee of five of the Senate, and their response displays vigor and asperity. I annex to this paper both documents.

The message of the President and the response of the Committee of the Senate occupied the thoughts of the last two days of the last Congress of the Confederate States. It ended March 15, 1865. The history of the remainder of this month was that of a busy time. The exchange of prisoners had been going on. Without reference to exact interchange, all of the prisoners accumulated in Richmond were sent away on the vessels. Some battles took place, in which the Confederates suffered disastrously, and on the 1st of April there was a defeat which was fatal and final, and the precursor and necessary cause of a capitulation within the week which followed.

Richmond was evacuated the 2d of April, and was captured on the 3d of April. I informed the Secretary of War that I should not leave Richmond, and that I should take an opportunity to see President Lincoln on the subject of peace and would be glad to have an authority to do so, but that I would do so if an occasion arose. President Lincoln came to the city on the 4th of April, in less than forty-eight hours from the departure of the President and his Cabinet. Richmond had experienced a great calamity from a conflagration. I represented the conditions to him and requested that no requisitions on the inhabitants be made of restraint of any sort save as to police and preservation of order; not to exact oaths, interfere with churches, &c. He assented to this. The General Weitzel and Military Governor Shepley cordially assenting.

On the following day I visited him on the Malvern gunboat on which he had come into Richmond upon the 4th. He had prepared a paper which he commented on as he read each clause. The paper was not signed nor dated. This paper he handed to me, and on the 13th of April 1 returned it to General Ord by direction of the President. I retained a copy as I informed that General I should do. This is a copy :—

"1. As to peace I have said before and now repeat that three things are indispensable. The restoration of the national authority throughout all the States.

"2. No receding by the Executive of the United

States on the slavery question from the position assumed thereon in the late annual message to Congress and in preceding documents.

"3. No cessation of hostilities short of an end of hostilities and the disbanding of all forces hostile to the government.

"That all propositions coming from those now in hostility to the government and not inconsistent with the foregoing, will be respectfully considered and passed upon in a spirit of sincere liberality. I now add that it seems useless for me to be more specific with those who will not say that they are ready for the indispensable terms, even on condition to be named by themselves. If there be any who are ready for those indispensable terms on any condition whatever let them say so, and state their conditions, so that such conditions can be distinctly known and considered. It is further added that the remission of confiscation being within the executive power, if the war be now further persisted in by those opposing the government, the making of confiscated property, at the least, to bear the additional cost will be insisted on; but that confiscations (except in case of third party intervening interests) will be remitted to the people of any State which shall now promptly, and in good faith, withdraw its troops and other supports from further resistance to the government. What is now said as to remission of confiscation has no reference to supposed property in slaves."

On the 13th of April, the day before the assassination of the President, General Ord addressed me a letter, stating that by the instructions of the President he wrote, that since the paper was written on the subject of reconvening the gentlemen who, under the insurrectionary government as the Legislature of Virginia, the object had in view and the convention of such gentlemen is unnecessary; he wishes the paper withdrawn. I sent to General Ord the only paper I had ever received, being that I have copied.

After the President had read and expounded the paper he delivered it to me. It was not dated nor signed, nor directed to me or other person. When he had concluded this he said he had been meditating a plan, but had come to no conclusion upon the subject; that he should not do so till he returned to City Point. That if he was satisfied he would write to General Weitzell.

This had reference to a convention of the Legislature which had been sitting during the preceding winter, and recognized the Confederate States. The President said: "He had a government in Virginia—the Pierrepont government. It had but a small margin, and he was not disposed to increase it. He wanted the very Legislature which had

6

been sitting 'up yonder'—pointing to the capitol —to come together and to vote to restore Virginia to the Union, and recall her soldiers from the Confederate army."

The suggestion came from the President, and its object was plainly stated. As the suggestion had some tolerance for the existing State governments, I was pleased to hear it, and strongly supported the suggestion. I told him "there had been discussions during the winter in respect to both peace and union; none could be found to make peace. Each man would now make his own peace." My opinion has been that his assassination was a very great calamity, and that this, among other calamities, would most probably have been averted had there been sober-minded views on the part of those charged with administration of affairs in the Confederate States.

It appears that Edwin M. Stanton was examined in relation to this intercourse before the committee appointed for the examination of charges preferred against President Johnson in 1867. He testified before that committee, "that President Lincoln went to the city of Richmond after its capture and some intercourse took place between him and Judge Campbell, formerly of the Supreme Court of the United States, and General Weitzell, which resulted in the call of the Rebel Legislature to Richmond. Mr. Lincoln on his return from Richmond reconsidered that matter."

The policy of undertaking to restore the government through the medium of rebel organizations was very much opposed by many persons, and very strongly and vehemently opposed by myself. I had several earnest conversations with Mr. Lincoln on the subject, and advised that any effort to reorganize the government should be under the Federal Government solely, and to treat the rebel organizations as null and void.

On the day preceding his death, a conversation took place between him, the Attorney-General and myself, upon the subject at the Executive mansion.

An hour or two afterwards, and about the middle of the afternoon, Mr. Lincoln came over to the War Department and renewed the conversation. After I had repeated my reasons against allowing the Rebel Legislatures to assemble, or the Rebel authorities to have any participation in the business of reorganization, he sat down at my desk and wrote a telegram to General Weitzell and handed it to me. "There," said he, "I think this will suit you." I told him no, it did not go far enough. That the members of the Legislature would probably come to Richmond; that General Weitzell ought to be directed to prohibit their assembling. He took up his pen again and made that addition to the telegram and signed it. He handed it to me. I said it was exactly right. It was transmitted immediately to General Weitzell, and was the last act ever performed by Mr. Lincoln in the War Department. General Ord had succeeded General Weitzell and communicated the intelligence to me. There was no sort of disappointment nor surprise at this proceeding. It was perfectly obvious that the dissolution of the Confederate States and government would immediately ensue the capture of the army.

The Last Message of the President of the Confederacy to Congress.

The following message was transmitted to Congress on Monday, 13th March, 1865:

To the Senate and House of Representatives of the Confederate States of America:

When informed on Thursday last that it was the intention of Congress to adjourn *sine die* on the ensuing Saturday, I deemed it my duty to request a postponement of the adjournment, in order that I might submit, for your consideration, certain matters of public interest, which are now laid before you. When that request was made, the most important measures that had occupied your attention during the session had not been so far advanced as to be submitted for executive action, and the state of the country had been so materially affected by the events of the last four months as to evince the necessity of further and more energetic legislation than was contemplated in November last.

Our country is now environed with perils which it is our duty calmly to contemplate. Thus alone can the measures necessary to avert threatened calamity be wisely devised and efficiently enforced.

Progress of the War.

Recent military operations of the enemy have been success-ful in the capture of some of our seaports, in interrupting some of our lines of communication, and in devastating large districts of our country. These events have had the natural effect of encouraging our foes and dispiriting many of our people. The capital of the Confederate States is now threat-ened, and is in greater danger than it has heretofore been during the war. The fact is stated without reserve or con-cealment as due to the people whose servants we are, and in whose courage and constancy entire trust is reposed; as due to you, in whose wisdom and resolute spirit the people have confided for the adoption of the measures required to guard them from threatened perils.

While stating to you that our country is in danger, I desire also to state my deliberate conviction that it is within our power to avert the calamities which menace us, and to secure the triumph of the sacred cause for which so much sac-rifice has been made, so much suffering endured, so many precious lives been lost. This result is to be obtained by for-titude, by courage, by constancy in enduring the sacrifices still needed; in a word, by the prompt and resolute devotion of the whole resources of men and money in the Confederacy to the achievement of our liberties and independence.

The measures now required, to be successful, should be prompt. Long deliberation and protracted debate over im-portant measures are not only natural, but laudable in repre-sentative assemblies under ordinary circumstances; but in moments of danger, when action becomes urgent, the delay thus caused is in itself a new source of peril. Thus it has unfortunately happened that some of the measures passed by you in pursuance of the recommendations contained in my message of November last have been so retarded as to lose much of their value, or have, for the same reason, been abandoned after being matured, because no longer applicable to our altered condition; and others have not been brought under examination. In making these remarks, it is far from my intention to attribute the loss of time to any other causes than those inherent in deliberative assemblies, but only urgently to recommend prompt action upon the measures now submitted. We'need for carrying on the war successfully, men and supplies for the army. We have both within our country sufficient to obtain success.

To obtain the supplies it is necessary to protect productive districts, guard our lines of communication by an increase in the number of our forces; and hence it results, that with a large augmentation of the number of men in the army, the facility of supplying the troops would be greater than with our recent reduced strength.

Supplies—Payment for them in Coin.

For the purchase of supplies now required, especially for the armies in Virginia and North Carolina, the treasury must be provided with means; and a modification in the impressment law is required. It has been ascertained, by examination, that we have within our reach a sufficiency of what is most needed for the army, and without having resource to the ample provision existing in those parts of the Confederacy with which our communication has been partially interrupted by hostile operations. But in some districts from which supplies are drawn, the inhabitants being either within the enemy's lines or in very close proximity, are unable to make use of Confederate treasury notes for the purchase of articles of prime necessity; and it is necessary that to some extent coin be paid in order to obtain supplies. It is therefore recommended that Congress devise the means for making available the coin within the Confederacy for the purpose of supplying the army. The officers of the supply department report that with two millions of dollars in coin, the armies in Virginia and North Carolina can be amply supplied for the remainder of the year; and the knowledge of this fact should suffice to insure the adoption of the measures necessary to obtain this moderate sum.

Impressments.

The impressment law, as it now exists, prohibits the public officers from impressing supplies without making payment of the valuation at the time of impressment. The limit fixed for the issue of treasury notes has been nearly reached, and the treasury cannot always furnish the funds necessary for prompt payment while the law for raising revenue which would have afforded means for diminishing, if not removing, this difficulty, was, unfortunately, delayed for several months, and has just been signed. In this condition of things, it is impossible to supply the army, although ample stores may exist in the country, whenever the owners refuse to give credit to the public officer. It is necessary that this restriction on the power of impressment be removed. The power is admitted to be objectionable, liable to abuse, and unequal in its operation on individuals; yet, all these objections must yield to absolute necessity. It is also suggested that the system of valuation now established ought to be radically changed.

The legislation requires in such cases of impressment, that the market price be paid; but there is really no market price in many cases, and then valuation is made arbitrarily and in a depreciated currency. The result is that the most extravagant prices are fixed, such as no one expects ever to be paid in coin. None believe that the Government can ever redeem in coin the obligation to pay fifty dollars a bushel for corn, or seven hundred dollars a barrel for flour. It would seem to be more just and appropriate to estimate the supplies impressed at their value in coin ; to give the obligation of the Government for the payment of the price in coin, with reasonable interest, or, at the option of the creditor, to return in kind the wheat or corn impressed, with a reasonable interest, also payable in kind; and to make the obligations thus issued receivable for all payments due in coin to the Government. Whatever be the value attached by Congress to these suggestions, it is hoped there will be no hesitation in so changing the law as to render it possible to supply the army in case of necessity for the impressment of provisions for that purpose.

The measure adopted to raise revenue, though liberal in its provisions, being clearly inadequate to meet the arrear of debt and the current expenditures, some degree of embarrassment in the management of the finances must continue to be felt. It is to be regretted, I think, that the recommendation of the Secretary of the Treasury, of a tax on agricultural income equal to the augmented tax on other incomes, payable in treasury notes, was rejected by Congress. This tax would have contributed materially to facilitate the purchase of provisions and diminish the necessity that is now felt for a supply of coin.

The Exemption Bill.

The measures passed by Congress during the session for recruiting the army and supplying the additional force needed for the public defence have been, in my judgment, insufficient, and I am impelled by a profound conviction of duty, and stimulated by a sense of the perils which surround our country, to urge upon you additional legislation upon this subject.

The bill for employing negroes as soldiers has not yet reached me, though the printed journals of your proceedings inform me of its passage. Much benefit is anticipated from this measure, though far less than would have resulted from its adoption at an earlier date, so as to afford time for their organization and instruction during the winter months.

The bill for diminishing the number of exempts has just

been made the subject of a special message, and its provisions are such as would add no strength to the army. The recommendation to abolish all class exemptions has not met your favor, although still deemed by me a valuable and important measure; and the number of men exempted by a new clause in the act just passed is believed to be quite equal to that of those whose exemption is revoked. A law of a few lines repealing all class exemptions would not only strengthen the forces in the field, but be still more beneficial by abating the natural discontent and jealousy created in the army by the existence of classes privileged by law to remain in places of safety while their fellow-citizens are exposed in the trenches and the field.

The Militia.

The measure most needed, however, at the present time, for affording an effective increase to our military strength, is a general militia law, such as the Constitution authorizes Congress to pass by granting to it power " to provide for organizing, arming, and disciplining the militia, and for governing such part of them as may be employed in the service of the Confederate States," and the further power " to provide for calling forth the militia to execute the laws of the Confederate States, suppress insurrections and repel invasions." The necessity for the exercise of this power can never exist if not in the circumstances which now surround us. The security of the States against any encroachment by the Confederate Government is amply provided by the Constitution, by " reserving to the States, respectively, the appointment of the officers, and the authority of training the militia according to the discipline prescribed by Congress."

A law is needed to prescribe not only how, and of what persons, the militia are to be organized, but to provide the mode of calling them out. If instances are required to show the necessity of such general law, it is sufficient to mention that, in one case, I have been informed by the Governor of a

7

State that the law does not permit him to call the militia from one county for service in another, so that a single brigade of the enemy could traverse the State, and devastate each county in turn, without any power on the part of the Executive to use the militia for effective defence; while in another State the Executive refused to allow the militia " to be employed in the service of the Confederate States," in the absence of a law for that purpose.

Suspension of the Habeas Corpus.

I have heretofore, in a confidential message to the two Houses, stated the facts that induced me to consider it necessary that the privilege of the writ of *habeas corpus* should be suspended. The conviction of the necessity of this measure has become deeper as the events of the struggle have been developed. Congress has not concurred with me in opinion. It is my duty to say that the time has arrived when the suspension of the writ is not simply advisable and expedient, but almost indispensable to the successful conduct of the war. On Congress must rest the responsibility of declining to exercise a power conferred by the Constitution as a means of public safety, to be used in periods of national peril resulting from foreign invasion. If our present circumstances are not such as were contemplated when this power was conferred, I confess myself at a loss to imagine any contingency in which this clause of the Constitution will not remain a dead letter.

With the prompt adoption of the measures above recommended, and the united and hearty coöperation of Congress and the people in the execution of the laws and the defence of the country, we may enter upon the present campaign with cheerful confidence in the result. And who can doubt the continued existence of that spirit and fortitude in the people, and of that constancy under reverses which alone are needed to render our triumph secure? What other resource remains available but the undying, unconquerable resolve to be free?

It has become certain beyond all doubt or question, that we must continue this struggle to a successful issue, or must make abject and unconditional submission to such terms as it shall please the conqueror to impose on us after our surrender. If a possible doubt could exist after the conference between our commissioners and Mr. Lincoln, as recently reported to you, it would be dispelled by a recent occurrence, of which it is proper that you should be informed.

The Peace Conference—Military Convention—Interview
Between Generals Longstreet and Ord.

Congress will remember that, in the conference above referred to, our commissioners were informed that the Government of the United States would not enter into any agreement or treaty whatever with the Confederate States, nor with any single State; and that the only possible mode of obtaining peace was by laying down our arms, disbanding our forces, and yielding unconditional obedience to the laws of the United States, including those passed for the confiscation of our property and the constitutional amendment for the abolition of slavery. It will further be remembered, that Mr. Lincoln declared that the only terms on which hostilities could cease were those stated in his message of December last, in which we were informed that, in the event of our penitent submission, he would temper justice with mercy, and that the question whether we should be governed as dependent territories, or permitted to have a representation in their Congress, was one on which he could promise nothing, but which would be decided by their Congress after our submission had been accepted.

It has not, however, been hitherto stated to you that, in the course of the conference at Fortress Monroe, a suggestion was made by one of our commissioners that the objections entertained by Mr. Lincoln to treating with the Government of the Confederacy, or with any separate State, might be avoided by substituting for the usual mode of negotiating through commissioners or other diplomatic agents the method sometimes employed of a military convention to be entered into by the commanding generals of the armies of the two belligerents. This he admitted was a power possessed by him, though it was not thought commensurate with all the questions involved. As he did not accept the suggestion when made, he was afterwards requested to reconsider his conclusion upon the subject of a suspension of hostilities, which he agreed to do, but said he had maturely considered of the plan, and had determined that it could not be done.

Subsequently, however, an interview with General Longstreet was asked for by General Ord, commanding the enemy's army of the James, during which General Longstreet was informed by him that there was a possibility of arriving at a satisfactory adjustment of the present unhappy difficulties by means of a military convention, and that if General Lee desired an interview on the subject it would not be declined, provided General Lee had authority to act. This communication was supposed to be in consequence of the suggestion above referred to, and General Lee, according to instructions, wrote to General Grant, on the second of this month, proposing to meet him for conference on the subject, and stating that he was vested with the requisite authority. General Grant's reply stated that he had no authority to accede to the proposed conference; that his powers extended only to making a convention on subjects purely of a military character, and that General Ord could only have meant that an interview would not be refused on any subject on which he (General Grant) had the right to act.

It thus appears, that neither with the Confederate authorities, nor the authorities of any State, nor through the commanding generals, will the Government of the United States treat or make any terms or agreement whatever for the cessation of hostilities. There remains then for us no choice but to continue this contest to a final issue; for the people of the

Confederacy can be but little known to him who supposes it possible they would ever consent to purchase at the cost of degradation and slavery, permission to live in a country garrisoned by their own negroes, and governed by officers sent by the conqueror to rule over them.

Conclusion.

Having thus fully placed before you the information requisite to enable you to judge of the state of the country, the dangers to which we are exposed, and the measures of legislation needed for averting them, it remains for me but to invoke your attention to the consideration of those means by which, above all others, we may hope to escape the calamities that would result from our failure. Prominent, above all others, is the necessity for cordial and earnest coöperation between all departments of government, State and Confederate, and all eminent citizens throughout the Confederacy. To you especially, as Senators and Representatives, do the people look for encouragement and counsel. To your action, not only in legislative halls, but in your homes, will their eyes be turned for the example of what is befitting men who, by willing sacrifices on the altar of freedom, show that they are worthy to enjoy its blessings.

I feel full confidence that you will concur with me in the conviction that your public duties will not be ended when you shall have closed the legislative labors of the session, but that your voice will be heard cheering and encouraging the people to that persistent fortitude which they have hitherto displayed, and animating them by the manifestation of that serene confidence which, in moments of public danger, is the distinctive characteristic of the patriot, who derives courage from his devotion to his country's destiny, and is thus enabled to inspire the like courage in others.

Thus united in a common and holy cause, rising above all selfish considerations, rendering all our means and faculties tributary to our country's welfare, let us bow submissively to the Divine will, and reverently invoke the blessing of our Heavenly Father, that as He protected and guided our sires when struggling in a similar cause, so He will enable us to guard safely our altars and our firesides, and maintain inviolate the political rights which we inherited.

JEFFERSON DAVIS.

RICHMOND, *March* 13, 1865.

REPORT OF THE SENATE COMMITTEE ON PRESIDENT DAVIS'S LAST MESSAGE.

The following is the report of the Senate Committee on the recent message of President Davis. It was read and adopted in secret session, and the seal of secresy removed on the 16th instant.

The select committee, to which was referred so much of the President's Message of the 13th instant as relates to the action of Congress during the present session, having duly considered the same, respectfully submit the following report:

The attention of Congress is called by the President to the fact that, for carrying on the war successfully, there is urgent need of supplies and men for the army.

The measures passed by Congress during the present session for recruiting the army are considered by the President inefficient; and it is said that the results of the law authorizing the employment of slaves as soldiers will be less than anticipated, in consequence of the dilatory action of Congress in adopting the measure. That a law so radical in its character, so repugnant to the prejudices of our people, and so intimately affecting the organism of society, should encounter opposition and receive a tardy sanction, ought not to excite surprise; but if the policy and necessity of the measure had been seriously urged on Congress by an Executive message, legislative action might have been quickened. The President, in no official communication to Congress, has recommended the passage of a law putting slaves into the army as soldiers, and the message under consideration is the first official information that such a law would meet his approval. The Executive message transmitted to Congress on the 7th of November last, suggests the propriety of enlarging the sphere of employment of the negro as a laborer, and for this purpose recommends that the absolute title to slaves be acquired by impressment, and, as an incentive to the faithful discharge of duty, that the slaves thus acquired be liberated, with the permission of the States from which they were drawn. In this connection the following language is used:

"If this policy should recommend itself to the judgment of Congress, it is suggested that, in addition to the duties heretofore performed by the slaves, they might be advantageously employed as *pioneer* and *engineer* laborers; and, in that event, that the number should be augmented to forty thousand. *Beyond this limit and these employments it does not seem to me desirable, under existing circumstances, to go.*"

In the same message the President further remarks:

"The subject is to be viewed by us, therefore, solely in the light of our policy and our social economy. *When so regarded, I must dissent from those who advise a general levy and arming the slaves for the duty of soldiers.*"

· It is manifest that the President, in November last, did not consider that the contingency had then arisen which would justify a resort to the extraordinary measure of arming our slaves. Indeed, no other inference can be deduced from the language used by him; for he says:

"These considerations, however, are rather applicable *to the improbable contingency of our need of resorting to this element of resistance than to our present condition.*"

The Secretary of War, in his report, under date of November 3d, seemed to concur in the opinion of the President when he said:

"While it is encouraging to know this resource for further

and future efforts is at our command, *my own judgment does not yet either perceive the necessity or approve the policy of employing slaves in the higher duties of soldiers."*

At what period of the session the President or Secretary of War considered the improbable contingency had arisen, which required a resort to slaves as an element of resistance, does not appear by any official document within the knowledge of your committee. Congress might well have delayed action on this subject until the present moment, as the President, whose constitutional duty it is "to give to the Congress information of the state of the Confederacy," has never asked, in any authentic manner, for the passage of a law authorizing the employment of slaves as soldiers. The Senate, however, did not wait the tardy movements of the President. On the 29th of December, 1864, the following resolution was adopted by the Senate in secret session :

" *Resolved,* That the President be requested to inform the Senate, in secret session, as to the state of the finances in connection with the payment of the troops; the means of supplying the munitions of war, transportation, and subsistence ; the condition of the army and the possibility of recruiting the same; the condition of our foreign relations, and whether any aid or encouragement from abroad is expected, or has been sought, or is proposed, so that the Senate may have a clear and exact view of the state of the country, and of its future prospects, and what measures of legislation are required."

In response to this resolution, the President might well have communicated to the Senate his views as to the necessity and policy of arming the slaves of the Confederacy as a means of public defence. No answer whatever has been made to the resolution. In addition to this, a joint committee was raised by Congress under a concurrent resolution adopted in secret session on the 30th of December, 1864. That committee, by the resolution creating it, was instructed, " by conference with the President, and by such other means as they shall deem proper, to ascertain what are our reliable means of public defence, present, and prospective."

A written report was made by the committee on January 25th, 1865; and although it had had a conference with the President, no allusion is made in the report to any suggestion by him that the necessities of the country required the employment of slaves as soldiers.   Under the circumstances, Congress, influenced, no doubt, by the opinion of General Lee, determined for itself the propriety, policy and necessity of adopting the measure in question.

The recommendations of the President to employ forty thousand slaves as cooks, teamsters, and as engineer and pioneer laborers, was assented to, and a law has been enacted at the present session for the purpose, without limit as to number.   All the measures recommended by the President to promote the efficiency of the army have been adopted except the entire repeal of class exemptions; and some measures not suggested by him—such as the creation of the office of General-in-Chief—were originated and passed by Congress, with a view to the restoration of public confidence and the energetic administration of military affairs.

On the subject of exemptions, the President in his message of November 7th, uses the following language :

"No pursuit nor position should relieve any one who is able to do active duty from enrolment in the army unless his functions or services are more useful to the defence of the country in another sphere.   But it is manifest that this cannot be the case with entire classes.   All telegraph operators, workmen in mines, professors, teachers, engineers, editors and employés of newspapers, journeymen printers, shoemakers, tanners, blacksmiths, millers, physicians, and numerous other classes mentioned in the laws cannot, in the nature of things, be either equally necessary in their several professions, nor distributed throughout the country in such proportions that only the exact numbers required are found in each locality."

The casual reader would infer that the laws, as they stood at the date of the message, exempted the classes enumerated by the President, as well as many other classes not mentioned

8

by him. Such is not the fact. The only class exemptions allowed by the laws then in force were the following : Ministers of religion ; superintendants and physicians of asylums for the deaf, dumb and blind, and of the insane; one editor for each newspaper, and such employés as the editor may certify on oath as indispensably necessary ; the public printers of the Confederate and State Governments, and their journeymen printers; one skilled apothecary in each apothecary store, who was doing business as such on the 10th of October, 1862 ; physicians over thirty years of age, and for the last seven years in practice; presidents and teachers of colleges, seminaries and schools, and the superintendents, physicians and nurses in public hospitals; certain mail-contractors and drivers of post-coaches ; certain officers and employés of railroad companies ; and certain agriculturists or overseers.

Officers of the State Governments are not properly included among the exempted classes, but it is conceded that Congress has no constitutional power to conscribe them as soldiers ; nor are Dunkards, Quakers, or other non-combatants regarded as belonging to class exemptions, because under the Act of June 7th, 1864, the exemption of these persons is subject to the control of the Secretary of War. The exemption of agriculturists or overseers, between the ages of eighteen and forty-five has been repealed at the present session. Tanners, shoemakers, millers, blacksmiths, telegraph operators and workmen in mines, enumerated by the President as among the classes exempted, are not now, and have not been since the passage of the Act of 17th February, 1864, exempted as a class. If railroad officers and employés, and State officers, who are not constitutionally subject to conscription, be excluded, the classes now exempted east of the Mississippi river embrace about nine thousand men—one-third of whom are physicians, and nearly another third are ministers of the gospel; the remaining third is principally composed of teachers, professors, printers and employés in newspaper offices and apothecaries.

In remarkable contrast to the number of persons relieved from military service by the exemptions above mentioned, the report of the Conscript Bureau exhibits the fact that, east of the Mississippi river, twenty-two thousand and thirty-five have been detailed by Executive authority. In consequence of this abuse of the power of detail, Congress, at its present session, passed an act revoking all details, and limiting the exercise of that power in the future. The third section of this act, exempting skilled artisans and mechanics from all military service, which is excepted to by the President, and which has since been repealed, was originally adopted in consequence of suggestions contained in the report of the Secretary of War. In alluding to the embarrassments encountered by the administrative bureaus, the Secretary says :

" In addition, they have been constrained, by the stringent legislation of Congress, to relinquish their most active and experienced agents and employés, and substitute for them more infirm and aged classes."

Again :

" Interferences of this kind are inevitably so prejudicial and disturbing, that it is hoped a well-devised and permanent plan of providing and retaining in continuous employment a sufficient number of artisans, experts, and laborers, for all essential operations, may be devised and established."

The truth is, that the bill originally introduced into the Senate exempting skilled artisans and mechanics was actually prepared in one of the bureaus of the War Department. Congress, therefore, had reason to suppose that it would meet the sanction of the Executive.

To conscribe the ministers of religion, and require them to obtain details to preach the Gospel, would shock the religious sentiment of the country, and inflict a greater injury on our cause than can be described. The conscription of the editors and of the printers necessary to the publication of newspapers, would destroy the independence of the press, and subject it to the control of the Executive Department of the

Government. The railroad officers and employés are as necessary to the prosecution of the war as soldiers in the field.. Physicians and apothecaries are essential to the health of the people, and no complaint has reached Congress of abuses in this class of exemptions. If the education of youth be regarded as conducive to the maintenance of society and the preservation of liberty, it is not perceived that the exemption of professors of colleges and teachers of schools can be justly censured. The Senate passed a bill containing a section repealing the exemption allowed to mail-contractors and drivers of post-coaches; but, at a subsequent stage of proceedings, and on the recommendation of a committee of Conference, based on the urgent remonstrances of the Postmaster General, the section alluded to was stricken out.

The subject of class exemptions was called to the attention of Congress by the Executive message of November last. It was carefully considered, and an act was passed expressive of the views of the Legislative Department of the Government. The message under consideration recurs to the same subject. It is to be regretted that the views of the Legislative Department of the Government have not met the favor of the Executive, and that he should deem it both necessary and proper to express dissatisfaction with the matured opinion of Congress.

It is true that Congress has failed to respond to the recommendation of the President to enact a general militia law. The subject was considered, and the failure to act was the result of deliberation. The conscription laws enacted by Congress have placed in the military service of the country all its able-bodied citizens between the ages of seventeen and fifty. The whole military material of the country, so far as legislation is concerned, is absorbed by the conscription acts. There is none left on which a militia law can operate, except the exempted classes, and the boys under seventeen, and the men over fifty years of age. It was deemed expedient to allow this material to remain subject to the control of the

State authorities for the purposes of local police, to aid in the arrest of deserters, and to enforce the administration of State laws.

It is also true that the President has recommended the passage of a law suspending the privilege of the writ of *habeas corpus.* The recommendation was the subject of a special message, in secret session. It occupied the attention of Congress for four or five weeks. After mature deliberation the measure was laid aside as unimportant and inexpedient. Spies can be arrested and tried summarily without suspending the writ of *habeas corpus.* Conspiracies, tending in any manner to the injury of our cause, were provided for by a special Act, passed at the present session, "to define and punish conspiracies against the Confederate States." The States of North Carolina, Georgia, and Mississippi had expressed, through their Legislatures, great repugnance to the past legislation of Congress suspending the writ, and a large portion of people throughout the country were arrayed against the policy of that legislation. It was deemed wise and prudent to conciliate opposition at a* time when dissensions are ruinous; and as the benefits to be derived from the suspension of the writ were conjectural, the deliberate judgment of Congress was expressed by its silence on the subject. It is to be regretted that the Executive does not concur in these views and again calls on Congress to revise its action, and to suspend the writ of *habeas corpus* as a measure "almost indispensable to the successful conduct of the war." If the facts stated in the confidential message alluded to by the President, be the basis of the opinion that the suspension of the writ " is indispensable to the successful conduct of the war," the Congress does not concur in that opinion. The writ has not been suspended since August last. It is not perceived that the military reverses of the country since that period were occasioned by the absence of the legislation asked for.

In regard to impressments, Congress, at the present session, has just passed a bill declaring that the terms "just compensation," as used in the Constitution, entitle the owner whose property is impressed to the market value thereof at the time and place of impressment. This legislation was considered necessary, in consequence of judicial decisions in some of the States, and because of the difficulty of procuring supplies on any other terms. Indeed, it was supposed that the Executive had reached the same conclusion, as the Commissary-General on the 20th of December, 1864, had advertised he would pay for supplies the price fixed by local appraisement; which is, in fact, the market price. The President, in his annual message of November last, did not call the attention of Congress to any difficulties attendant upon the execution of the impressment laws. The present message, for the first time during this session, suggests modifications of these laws; and the recommendations of the President will doubtless receive the respectful consideration of Congress. It may well be doubted, however, whether the present specie value, payable in the future, will induce the owner of property to part with it; and whether the passage of such a measure would not result in a general concealment of provisions, and consequent starvation of the army.

It is apprehended by the President that some degree of embarrassment in the management of the finances will be felt in consequence of the inadequate provisions made by Congress; and it is intimated that some of the measures recommended by him were so retarded as to lose much of their value; and others after being matured, were, for the same reason abandoned, because no longer applicable to our altered condition. The only financial measure abandoned after being matured was the currency bill, recommended by the Secretary of the Treasury and indorsed by the President in his Annual Message. It may be remarked that the failure to enact any fiscal measure, which has not sufficient vitality to render it valuable and applicable for the short space of four months, does not deserve much regret. The currency bill was recommended to Congress, and based on the condition the finances presented by the President in his message, and by the Secretary of the Treasury in his report. It was abandoned without regret, because, at a subsequent period of the session, it was ascertained that the arrears of public debt constituting cash demands on the Treasury exceeded, by nearly four hundred millions, the amount originally reported to Congress by the Secretary of the Treasury. The currency bill contemplated the reduction of the currency to one hundred and fifty millions by a conversion of treasury notes into tithe certificates, payable after the war, and by an annual application of a portion of the taxes in the nature of a sinking fund. The treasury notes received for the tithe certificates were to be cancelled. The military reverses, which impaired the credit of the Government to such an extent as to destroy the salability of any of its bonds, left little hope that treasury notes would be exchanged for tithe certificates. As soon as the enormous increase in the arrears of the debt was discovered, as above mentioned, all idea of reducing the currency was abandoned as impracticable. For these reasons, the committee of conference having charge of the currency bill agreed to abandon it as a useless pledge of future resources without corresponding present advantage. Indeed, if the bill had been passed the first day of the session it would have expired from inanition on the 9th of January, 1865, the day on which the Secretary of the Treasury reported to Congress the deficit of four hundred millions, and recommended an increase of taxes to meet it.

The tax-bill is regarded by the President as liberal, though inadequate. No nation on earth ever conducted a protracted war by resources derived from taxation alone. The message intimates a regret that the recommendation by the Secretary of the Treasury of a tax on agricultural income equal to the augmented tax on other income, payable in treasury notes, was rejected by Congress. This is evidently a mistake, as it assumes there has been an increase of taxes on other than agricultural incomes. The present income taxes are those laid by the Act of April, 1863, as amended and reënacted on the 17th of February, 1864. To require the agriculturist to pay a tax on the income derived from his farm in addition to the one-tenth of his gross productions, and the property tax of nine per cent. *ad valorem,* would be manifestly unjust and oppressive. After the delivery of his title, to tax the income of the agriculturist derived from the property producing the title, would leave little for family subsistence, for the purchase of supplies necessary for carrying on his agricultural operations, and for the payment of the *ad valorem* tax on his property. Congress, therefore, did not concur in the recommendation of the Secretary of the Treasury, believing it to be highly inexpedient. The recommendations of the Secretary of the Treasury have, in the main, received the approbation of Congress, and every disposition has been manifested to coöperate with him. The tax-bill adopted very nearly approximates the rate devised by him. He recommended ten per cent. on property. Congress has imposed a tax of nine per cent. A new foreign loan was authorized in secret session, at his request, without any limitation on his authority except as to the amount. A transfer of certain sterling funds abroad was, by joint resolution, directed to be made from the Navy to the Treasury. Efforts were made to raise specie. A bill was passed in the Senate, in secret session, to accomplish that object by the sale of certain licenses. It is understood the bill was defeated in the House of Representatives by the acquiescence, if not at the instigation, of the Secretary of the Treasury. It appears from the correspondence submitted to Congress that the Secretary of War, as early as the 18th of February, notified the President of the embarrassed condition of his department; and it is to be regretted that the Executive deliberated on, and postponed for so long a period as twenty days, the communication of that information to Congress. If loss of time be a vice inherent in deliberative assemblies, promptitude is a great virtue in Executive action. There is every disposition on the part of Congress to comply with the recommendations of the President, and some means of raising the coin desired will, no doubt, be devised. It is unfortunate that the necessity for coin in the Commissary Department was not made known until the message under consideration was received. The use of coin in one department of the Government is calculated to superinduce the necessity for its use in all other departments; hence the policy of the proposed measure, in a financial view, is very questionable. The necessity for supplies, however, overrides all other considerations. If practicable, it would be wiser to employ the specie in the purchase of treasury notes, and then use the notes to obtain supplies.

Nothing is more desirable than concord and cordial co-operation between all departments of Government. Hence your committee regret that the Executive deemed it necessary to transmit to Congress a message so well calculated to excite discord and dissension. But for the fact that the success of the great struggle in which the country is engaged depends as much on the confidence of the people in the Legislative as in the Executive Department of the Government, the message would have been received without comment. Your committee would have preferred silence. It has been induced to an opposite course, because they believe Congress would be derelict in its duty to permit its legitimate and constitutional influence to be destroyed by Executive admonitions, such as those contained in the message under consideration, without some public exposition of its conduct.

Respectfully submitted.

> JAMES L. ORR, *Chairman,*
> THOMAS J. SEMMES,
> W. A. GRAHAM,
> A. T. CAPERTON,
> JOHN W. C. WATSON.

9

The last message of the President of the Confederate States to their Congress is divided by
paragraphs with titles, and is comprehensive in
its review of the public condition.—Supplies; Payment for them in Coin; Impressment of Supplies;
The Exemption Bill; The Militia; Suspension of
the *Habeas Corpus;* the Peace Conference; Military
Convention, are the subjects which engaged the
attention of the Government at this moment.
There was an expression of confidence in the
triumph of the Confederate arms; the subjects to
be considered would probably require time and
thought.   The reply of the Committee of the
Senate was dissentient and defensive.

It was unquestionably true that during the last
two years of the existence of the Confederate
Government that the opinions promulgated and
sustained as to the military condition, under its
influence, has been criticised with disfavor abroad
as neither accurate nor intelligent.   " That the
Government acted under thoroughly false views
of the military situation," is the opinion of perhaps the most eminent of the military critics of
Great Britain.   During these years there had been
improvement in the armies of the Federal Government, in discipline, the capacity of the officers,
their numbers, and in all of the arrangements for
subsistence, equipment, and the quality of the
arms.   In nearly all of these the Southern armies

had deteriorated, and the disproportion had ceased to exist, if any had existed.

The consequences were not sufficiently recognized and considered, and when the campaign of 1864 terminated, it is apparent that the Confederate armies in Virginia were greatly exhausted and unfitted for a similar campaign. The deterioration increased during the winter from the urgent efforts made to recruit the armies from those who had been exempt, and from the privations imposed upon families through the absence of the male members.

The detention of so many as prisoners, and the confinement of the sick contributed to further depression. General Lee communicated from time to time specimens of these letters, and stated the effects upon the *morale* of the army. Still these did not serve to convince the Civil Department. The Vice-President of the Confederate States told me that it was philosophically impossible to reconstitute a Union so disrupted, as we journeyed to Hampton Roads, and the hope of European intervention was a dream of the Secretary of State that proved all a dream.

General Lee has communicated in the letter addressed to the Secretary of War, dated about the 10th of March, and sent as part of the " Secret Message " on the 13th to Congress : " The situation is full of peril and difficulty, and requires prompt action." "If my situation is not greatly improved, I can neither hold my lines before Richmond, neither can I remove with my army from them." I have quoted from this letter. I have confined my writing to the disclosure of facts, and only include such as I am able to verify. I have had no purpose to sit in judgment on any one of the persons mentioned, nor to comment on the facts contained in this history.

JOHN A. CAMPBELL.

A TREATISE ON THE LAW

RELATING TO THE

CUSTODY OF INFANTS.

By LEWIS HOCHHEIMER, of the Baltimore Bar.

I volume, 8vo., 250 pages, $3.50

WASHINGTON LAW REPORTER.

This book is far outside of the class known as made books. It covers a topic daily arising, one which is troublesome to the bar, as well as to society, and it covers it so well that he who has anything to do with questions which involve the charge of infants in any of the relations with the law, will find his work easier, and have a sense of relief after reference to it. The book belongs to that topical class which the profession must have as practice grows upon them, and as the whole volume of property, passes through probate in each generation, the need of such becomes greater. It is divided into ten chapters, which treat: I. On the nature and limitation of the right of custody. II. Interference of courts of chancery in questions of custody. III and IV. The same upon writs of *habeas corpus*. V. The remedy by *habeas corpus*. VI. Probate and testamentary guardians. VII. Disposal of the custody upon the application for divorce. VIII. Illegitimate children. IX. Apprentices. X. Juvenile institutions.

Appendix.—Forms of returns to writs of *habeas corpus*.

The chapters are subdivided into sections; these again have sub-heads, all clearly divided and well defined. The indexing is well done, attention being had not alone to the topic in, but its division and subdivision. It is very full both of English and American cases, as well as to the elementary writers. Even citations are given from minor courts, which are reported only in local law journals, showing that the author has given much labor to its construction, and one gets a sense that it shows him nearly if not quite all the authority there is up to its date, viz., September 15, 1887. The matter is well and clearly written, covers 222 pages, and is well printed on excellent paper, and well bound in law sheep. The index to cases is very copious and as in additions to the page citings is a real help. We might, if inclined, criticise by saying that we wish Mr. Hochheimer had included the other subjects of guardianship, viz., insane persons, drunkards, spendthrifts, etc., etc., and that he may be encouraged to see his way clear to do so in the near future.

PITTSBURG LEGAL JOURNAL.

This is a compilation of the law as it has been declared in the hundreds of cases of *habeas corpus*, involving the custody of children that have been passed upon by the courts of this country and Great Britain, with an exposition of the principles which underly and govern the whole subject-matter. The work appears to be carefully and well prepared.

BALTIMORE SUNDAY NEWS.

The above treatise, by a well-known member of the legal profession of our city, is a valuable addition to legal literature. It is comprehensive in its character, embracing the entire scope of common law doctrines in relation to the interesting and important topic discussed. The subject in all its bearings is thoroughly considered and the treatise throughout bears evidence of intelligent and exhaustive investigation of a branch of municipal law with which few, even among the most learned jurists, are entirely familiar. The treatise is worthy to take rank as a standard work.

The book is gotten up in a style of type, binding and general mechanical features of such superior excellence as to reflect the highest credit on the publishers.

JOHN MURPHY & CO., Law Publishers, Baltimore.

www.ingramcontent.com/pod-product-compliance
Lightning Source LLC
Chambersburg PA
CBHW032344020726
47499CB00009B/3169